TROUBLE AT THE WATERING HOLE

The Adventures of Emo and Chickie

Gregg F. Relyea and Joshua N. Weiss

Illustrated by Vikrant Singh

About the Authors

Mr. Relyea is a mediator, negotiation teacher, and lawyer. In addition to helping people resolve their legal and commercial disputes with mediation, arbitration and other forms of dispute resolution, Mr. Relyea teaches negotiation at the University of San Diego School of Law and the University of California, San Diego. Mr. Relyea is a member of the Panel of Distinguished Mediators for the American Arbitration Association.

Joshua N. Weiss, Ph.D., is the Co-Founder of the Global Negotiation Initiative at Harvard Law School and a Senior Fellow at the Harvard Negotiation Project. Dr. Weiss is also the creator and Director of the Masters Degree in Leadership and Negotiation at Bay Path University.

Both Mr. Relyea and Dr. Weiss have authored numerous publications about negotiation and mediation in professional journals, podcasts, and other publications/media.

Trouble at the Watering Hole

Coloring Book

Copyright © 2017 by Gregg F. Relyea and Joshua N. Weiss.

Resolution
Press

Illustration and Composition by Vikrant Singh (ART FACT INDIA)

Coloring Book Art by Jonathan Short

ISBN-978-0-9982423-2-3

Praise for "Trouble at the Watering Hole"

From His Holiness The Dalai Lama, Dharamsala, India

The only sensible and intelligent way of resolving differences in today's world is through dialogue in a spirit of compromise and reconciliation. Dialogue, through which we learn to listen to other points of view, is the way to build greater trust and transparency, and is the foundation of lasting friendship. Everyone from small children up to political leaders have to understand that violence and conflict are counterproductive, that they are not a realistic way to solve our problems . . .

"Trouble at the Watering Hole" makes a valuable contribution to such educational efforts by imagining how animals deal with trouble round the watering hole. It is a vivid scene that children will easily understand. I congratulate the authors for their keen appreciation of the importance of finding ways to educate children so they grow up learning not to lash out at the first sign of conflict, but to approach problems more reasonably. Genuine peace and reconciliation, whether in relation to ourselves or in relation to others, comes about through taking an understanding, respectful and non-violent approach to the challenges we face.

From Dr. Daniel Shapiro: Director, Harvard International Negotiation Program

Everywhere we turn, it seems that youth are being exposed to the glorification of insult and violence, whether on social media or television, at the cinema or the toy-store lined with plastic guns and action figures. While it is useful for kids to learn about the complexity of human nature, there's a clear and desperate need for resources to educate children in peaceful methods of conflict resolution. This is why I was thrilled to read Trouble at the Watering Hole, a charming children's book by conflict resolution experts Gregg Relyea and Joshua Weiss. Through a simple story, the book embeds key skills children can use to resolve everyday conflicts.

From Niranjan Bhatt: President, Association of Indian Mediators (2000-2016) and Founder and Managing Trustee of AMLEAD (Institute for Arbitration, Mediation and Legal Education and Development), Gujarat, India

"Trouble at the Watering Hole" is a landmark contribution to the field of conflict resolution. A difficult subject has been brilliantly reduced to first principles for young readers. It will lead the younger generation to a more peaceful society. "Trouble" also can be incorporated at an advanced level in train-the-trainers programs. The parent-teacher manual is a superb way of elaborating the practical skills used in conflict resolution.

From Sriram Panchu: Founder, Indian Centre for Mediation and Dispute Resolution, India

It's a powerful message to convey to children - that they can end disputes by talking, that they can themselves ask the right questions and find the right answers, and that they can retain friendships. In a society where conflict is on the rise and is increasingly disabling, imparting and imbibing this message is a sign of hope.

From Hitoshi Suzuki: Co-Author of *The Settling Brain* and Professor (2007-2015) and Lecturer, Tokai University, Japan

It will be a more peaceful planet if every child reads this book when they are very young. It should be required reading for every student in school. The story will stimulate and awaken the better nature of people to be cooperative, reciprocal, and altruistic, at the youngest ages.

From Kenneth Cloke: Author of *Mediating Dangerously: The Frontiers of Conflict Resolution*

Conflicts begin at birth, and so should our skills in collaborative negotiation and conflict resolution. But how do we teach children diverse, age-appropriate ways of responding to conflict without either talking down to them or expecting them to act like professional mediators? This highly useful approach combines simple storytelling with a well-informed guide for teachers and parents covering skills for all ages, allowing teachers, parents and children to learn the same techniques, and practice them together.

From Laila Ollapally: Founder, Center for Advanced Mediation Practice, Bangalore, India

In this world of strife and violence, "Trouble at the Watering Hole" is telling our children a story of collaboration and deeper understanding. Imprinting peace on impressionable minds. My congratulations to Gregg Relyea and Josh Weiss.

From Winston Siu, Chairman of G2G Mediation Centre Limited (Hong Kong), Family and General Mediator, Mediation Course Trainer and Mediator Accreditation Assessor

Congratulations! The children's story with the training manual is a wonderful and effective way to let children acquire skills to resolve disputes, and to repair/enhance relationships. I can envision a more harmonious world, full of positive energy due to the impressive work of the authors.

From Roy Cheng: Author of *Getting to Harmony* and Founder of the Hong Kong Institute of Mediation

Most children have experienced the use of aggression and an "I'm right--you're wrong" approach to resolving conflict. As they grow, they internalize these approaches and continue to use them into adulthood. This book and manual will help children, as well as parents and teachers, understand interest-based negotiation and how to negotiate in a constructive and amicable way.

To Agastya and all the little ones of the world
who can face conflicts
--both small and large--
using timeless and proven skills.
--Gregg Relyea

To my three daughters Kayla, Aylee, and Talya:
you bring an abundance of light into my world
as well as a little heat so I can keep practicing how to
try to deal with conflict effectively.
--Joshua N. Weiss

Emo rolled and splashed the way brown bear cubs do at the edge of the watering hole.

Emo's Mama watched from a nearby clearing.

The summer sun was high. It was naptime in the forest.

Emo made his way to dry ground and dropped, PLOP!, on his back.

Emo's best friend, Chickie, a red-breasted robin perched in a pine tree above Emo.

"What a lucky bear I am!" Emo declared. "My belly's full, my best friend's with me, and Mama's close by to make sure I'm safe. Could it be any better?"

Emo's eyes grew heavy as the clouds changed shape.

Emo was almost asleep when loud screeches startled him. He sprang upright and jumped in the water.

Dazed and confused, Emo shook his head, "What's all that noise? What's wrong? So long naptime!"

Chickie agreed, "So long, peace and quiet."

Once again, the forest animals were fighting with each other.

"This water's mine!" snorted Moose.

"NO! It's MINE!" screeched Red Deer.

"It belongs to ME!" Gray Wolf howled and hollered.

The two friends moved behind a bush so they could get a closer look. Chickie flew down to ride on Emo's shoulder. From behind a bush they watched Moose stomp and splash. Red Deer splashed back, kicking her sharp hooves high, while Gray Wolf punched the water, growling and showing his sharp fangs.

Little Beaver, his mouth filled with twigs and branches, scurried in between the fir trees and pine.

Mosquitoes swarmed everywhere, buzzing loudly.

"Chickie," Emo said, "Isn't there anything we can do? There doesn't seem to be an end to all this fighting and arguing. Besides, I need my nap!"

Emo crept closer to the animals in the water. He took two, then three deep, deep breaths before he spoke.

"Excuse me, Mr. Moose, but my friend and I were thinking. Maybe it would help if you took a time-out."

Chickie chimed in, "Emo means calm down."

"You know, cool off," Emo added.

"And exactly what good would that do?" Moose shook water from his antlers.

Emo swallowed hard. "Then you could listen to each other."

"LISTEN?" Moose thundered. Water bursts swirled.

Chickie puffed out his chest. "Yes, listen," he said. Emo wiggled both ears to make sure they got the point.

"You could take turns talking, asking questions of each other," Chickie said. "That way, each one of you can explain what matters most to you."

Moose stood tall and lowered his huge pointed antlers for an attack. "There's nothing to talk about! I'm the largest and the strongest animal in this forest!" he announced. "So the water should be mine whenever I want it!"

"Hey! Wait a minute!" Gray Wolf howled. "I'm the cleverest animal in the forest. So the water should be mine!"

Red Deer kicked her sharp hooves and hollered, "I've been coming to this watering hole longer than any of you. By rights, the water belongs to me!"

Mosquitoes swarmed and circled. They claimed the water, too.

Meanwhile, Little Beaver ran quickly through the trees with his branches and twigs.

Emo raised his paw. "Whoa!" he said. "You're not listening to each other!"

"Let's cool down again," Chickie advised. "And this time, try listening to the reasons you each need this water."

Red Deer stomped off and lay beneath a shady pine tree.

"Could Emo and Chickie be right?" she asked herself. A cool breeze calmed her. "We all need the water but I wonder if we need it for different reasons."

Red Deer rose and joined Moose and Gray Wolf. "I want to understand, can we talk about why and when each of us needs the water?" she asked.

"Come to think of it," Gray Wolf said, "I only need the water at night when I roam."

"And me," Moose said, "I only need the water in the daytime when I eat grass and get thirsty."

Red Deer paused, breathing in the evergreen. "I must admit," she finally said, "I get most of my water from licking moss from tree leaves and rain and melting snow. I can use the watering hole any time of day."

The mosquitoes buzzed loudly. It turns out they only needed water at dusk and at dawn, to drink and lay their eggs.

Emo shook his stubby tail. "Naptime, here I come!" he whispered.

"Now isn't this better?" Chickie asked the animals. "First, you took time to cool down. Then you *talked about the things that really mattered* most and you *listened carefully* to each other, so you finally could get to the heart of the problem."

Emo agreed. "Does it help knowing that you each use the watering hole, but at different times and for different reasons?"

"Sure," said Moose.

"Certainly," said Red Deer.

"Of course," said Gray Wolf, "except..."

He pointed to the watering hole. "No matter **WHEN** or **WHY** we need it, this hole **NEEDS** to be even bigger! There's not enough water for all of us."

Chickie shook his head and looked at Emo, who was shaking his head too while he watched the sun move lower in the sky.

Emo sighed.

"So long, naptime. So long, peace and quiet."

Red Deer slumped her shoulders, fearing the animals would lose everything and start fighting again. Out of the corner of her eye, she spotted Little Beaver, who was busy piling twigs across a nearby creek to build a dam. An idea popped into Red Deer's head.

"Mr. Beaver, do you think you could turn some of the water from the creek toward the watering hole? You could keep your dam and there would be more water for us."

Little Beaver agreed, but he couldn't do all the work himself.

Moose shouted, "Hop on my back, Little Beaver, and we'll make the work go faster!"

"And I'll run along beside you," Gray Wolf howled, "to protect you from danger!"

The mosquitoes buzzed their approval. They'd wait beside Red Deer. All would guard the watering hole, except...

HONK! HONK! HONK!...in the middle of their brain-storming, a noisy flock of thirsty honking Herons landed in the water!

"*Uh, oh!*" Emo and Chickie cried. "Here we go again."

Red Deer took a deep breath, gathering her thoughts.

"Excuse me, Mr. Heron," she asked the tallest of the group, "but would you mind telling me why you need our water?"

"Oh, we're just stopping for a minute or two, for a quick drink," he answered. "We're on our way South."

Red Deer spied clear, fresh creek water flowing into the over-flowing watering hole, thanks to Little Beaver.

"Perfect," Red Deer offered. "Mr. Heron and friends, be our guest."

At last, peace and quiet returned to the watering hole. There was just enough afternoon sun left in the day for Emo's long-awaited nap. The warm breeze wrapped Emo in a soft blanket of air.

Emo could finally have his nap and he drifted off into a deep and restful sleep with his best friend, Chickie, by his side .

CPSIA information can be obtained
at www.ICGtesting.com
Printed in the USA
BVHW02s0757041018
529198BV00012B/216/P

9 780998 242309